PRINCE RIBBIT

For Tony and Lisa – J.E.

For my children, my true princes – P.B.

First published 2016 by Macmillan Children's Books
an imprint of Pan Macmillan Limited
20 New Wharf Road, London N1 9RR
Associated companies throughout the world
www.panmacmillan.com

ISBN 978-1-4472-8379-9 (HB)
ISBN: 978-1-4472-8432-1 (PB)

Text copyright © Jonathan Emmett 2016
Illustrations copyright © Poly Bernatene 2016
Moral rights asserted.
You can find out more about Jonathan Emmett's books at
www.scribblestreet.co.uk

1 3 5 7 9 8 6 4 2

A CIP catalogue record for this book is available from the British Library.

Printed in China

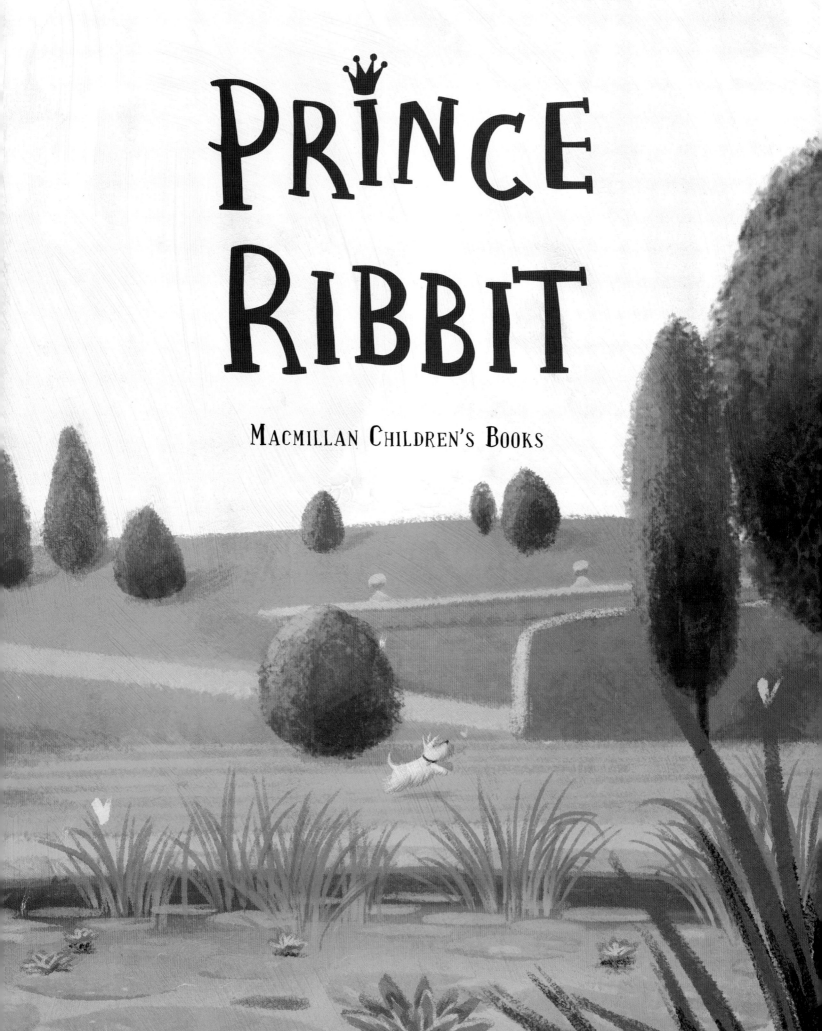

Jonathan Emmett

Poly Bernatene

PRINCE RIBBIT

MACMILLAN CHILDREN'S BOOKS

"And so the Princess and the Frog Prince got married and lived happily ever after," read Princess Arabella, closing the book with a satisfied sigh.

Princess Lucinda frowned, "That silly girl treated the Frog Prince so badly, she was lucky to marry him." "If I ever met a talking frog, I wouldn't make the same mistake," agreed Arabella.

Princess Martha rolled her eyes. She liked facts more than fairy tales and real frogs more than enchanted ones. She'd heard a real frog croaking in the royal pond, but she could never spot him.

He's a clever little thing, thought Martha.

Martha was right, the frog was very clever indeed. He often listened in on the sisters' stories and the more he heard of princes and princesses, the more he longed to live like one.

The frog dreamed of sleeping in a soft bed, eating fine foods and wearing a beautiful crown, and he'd just come up with a clever plan to make his dream come true.

"EEEYUCK!

Go away, you slimy little beast!"
shrieked Arabella and Lucinda as
the frog hopped out in front of them.

But instead of leaping into
the pond, the frog cleared
his throat and spoke.

"Allow me to introduce myself," said the cunning frog, "my name is Prince Ribbit."

Arabella and Lucinda stared, open mouthed, but Martha was delighted!
"It's a **FROG**," she shouted. "**A TALKING FROG!**"

"A jealous wizard turned me into a frog because I was so astonishingly handsome!" said Prince Ribbit. "If only there was a way to break the spell."

"But there is," cried Lucinda. "It's in this book! You just need to be looked after by a pretty princess like me!"

"Or a pretty princess like **ME!**" said Arabella. "And then you'll turn back into your old astonishingly handsome self and we can live happily ever after!"

Lucinda and Arabella took Prince Ribbit back to
the palace and gave him whatever he wanted.

Lucinda let him
sleep on her pillow ...

...while Arabella let him
eat from her plate.

But the more Princess Martha saw of the frog, the more suspicious she became.

"Why are you making such a fuss of him?" she asked
as Prince Ribbit hopped around the dinner table.

"Because he's an enchanted prince," said Arabella,
"and that's how you break the spell!"

"Just because it's in a book, it doesn't
mean it's true," said Martha.

And with that she went to the Royal Library, to find out the truth about frogs.

"A mummy frog lays eggs," she explained to her sisters.
"Then the eggs turn into tadpoles, and the tadpoles turn into frogs.
But frogs don't EVER turn into princes!"

"Just because it's in a book, it doesn't mean it's true," replied her sisters.

So the princesses continued to pamper Prince Ribbit.

They let him sleep in
the biggest, softest bed . . .

...and gave him the finest
clothing and a beautiful new crown.

Martha was the only person who saw
Prince Ribbit for what he really was.

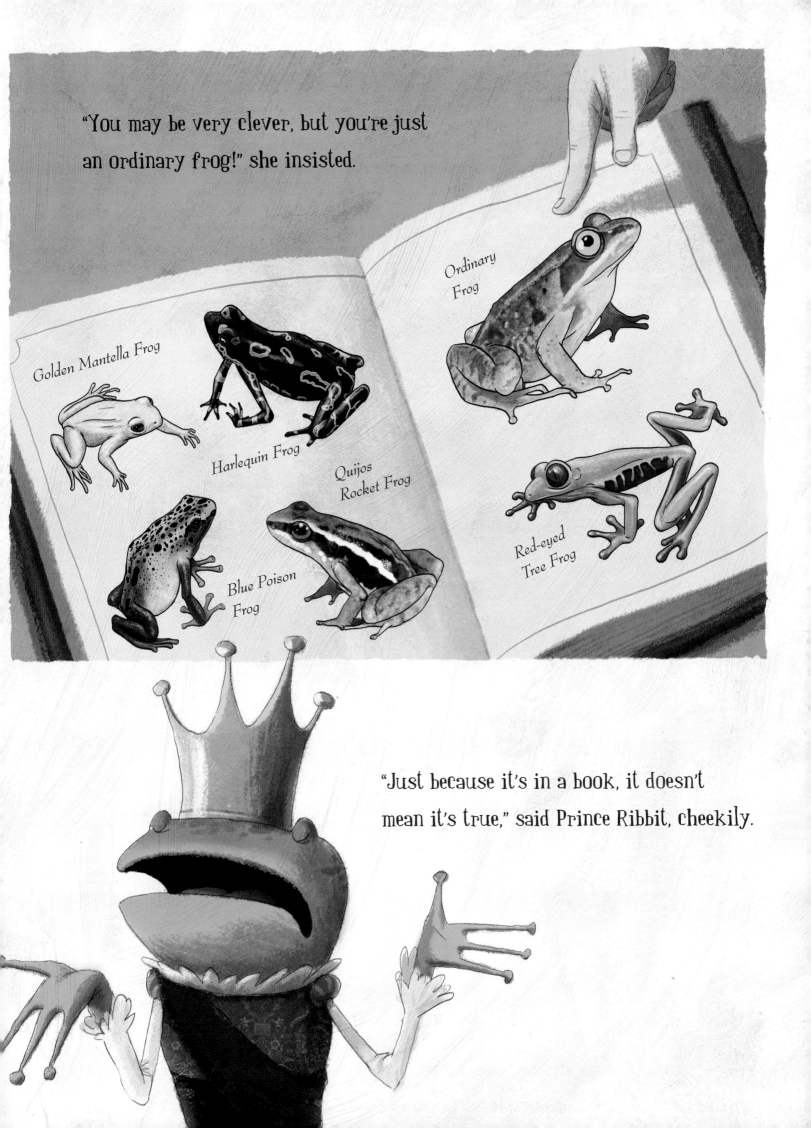

"You may be very clever, but you're just an ordinary frog!" she insisted.

Ordinary Frog

Golden Mantella Frog

Harlequin Frog

Quijos Rocket Frog

Blue Poison Frog

Red-eyed Tree Frog

"Just because it's in a book, it doesn't mean it's true," said Prince Ribbit, cheekily.

This is hopeless, thought Martha. My sisters will never believe me, no matter how many books of facts I show them. But I suppose I'm just as bad, I never look at their story books. Perhaps I should!

So Martha gathered a big pile of fairy tales and began to read.

She was surprised to find that, while stories might not be true, they were often funny, exciting and INSPIRING.

And after Martha had read them all, she knew exactly how to deal with Prince Ribbit.

"If you really are an enchanted prince, why hasn't the spell been broken yet?" asked Martha the next morning.

Prince Ribbit shifted uneasily in his little golden throne and adjusted his beautiful crown.

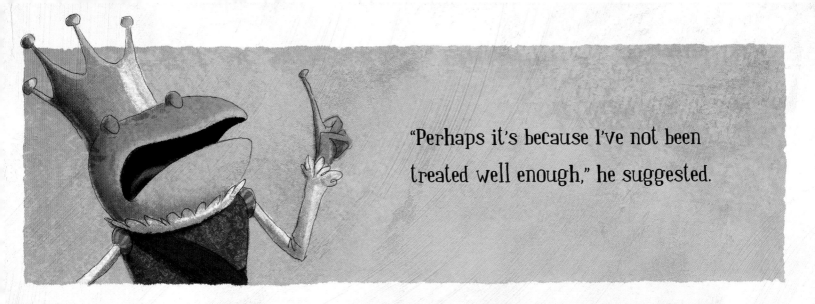

"Perhaps it's because I've not been treated well enough," he suggested.

"You seem very well treated to me!" said Martha. "I think it's time to try something different. What's the one thing that will always break an evil spell?"

"TRUE LOVE'S KISS!"

said Arabella and Lucinda excitedly.

"Me first!" said Princess Arabella, planting a big wet smacker on Prince Ribbit's clammy cheek.

"You don't love him as much as I do," said Princess Lucinda, snatching the frog from her sister and squashing his face in a passionate smooch.

But no matter how many kisses they gave him, Prince Ribbit remained very much a frog. And in the end both princesses realised that this was all he'd ever been and all he'd ever be.

"I suppose I should go back to my pond," sighed the frog, taking off his beautiful crown. But he looked so sad that Martha couldn't help feeling sorry for him.

"Please don't go," she said kindly. "Any animal smart enough to fool my sisters would be fun to have around. And while I might not want a handsome prince as a husband, I'd LOVE to have a clever frog as a friend!"

And she picked up the frog and gave him a gentle kiss.

The instant Martha kissed him, there was a huge puff of pink smoke and the frog turned into a handsome young prince.

In fact, he was **SO** handsome that Martha decided that she **DID** want to marry him after all. So she jumped into his arms and they both lived happily ever after!

And if that's not the ending you were expecting, then remember . . .

...just because it's in a book, it doesn't mean it's true!